D0814440

Flowering Inferno:
Tales of Sinking Hearts

Flowering Inferno: Tales of Sinking Hearts

by

Rima de Vallbona

Translated by

Lillian Lorca de Tagle

LATIN AMERICAN LITERARY REVIEW PRESS
SERIES: DISCOVERIES
PITTSBURGH, PENNSYLVANIA
1994

The Latin American Literary Review Press publishes Latin American creative writing under the series title *Discoveries*, and critical works under the series title *Explorations*.

Library of Congress Cataloging-in-Publication Data

Vallbona, Rima de,
[Infiernos de la mujer y algo más. English]
Flowering inferno : tales of sinking hearts / by Rima de Vallbona ; translated by Lillian Lorca de Tagle.
p. cm. -- (Discoveries)
ISBN 0-935480-64-1
I. Title. I. Series.
PQ7489.2.V3I6413 1994
863--dc20 93-39645
CIP

Cover illustration by Nélida Petrucelli. Cover design by Mary Lisa Pallo. Book design by Barbara Alsko.

The paper used in this publication meets the minimum requirements of the American National Standard for Permanence of Paper for Printed Library Materials Z39.48-1984. ♾

Flowering Inferno: Tales of Sinking Hearts may be ordered directly from the publisher:

Latin American Literary Review Press
121 Edgewood Avenue
Pittsburgh, PA 15218
Tel (412) 371-9023 • Fax (412) 371-9025

ACKNOWLEDGEMENTS

This project is supported in part by grants from the National Endowment for the Arts in Washington, D.C., a federal agency, and the Commonwealth of Pennsylvania Council on the Arts.

CONTENTS

My deepest gratitude to my daughter, Marisa Vallbona, who put so much love, effort, and time into editing this translation of *Los infiernos de la mujer y algo más....*

R.R.V

To my father, Ferdinand Hermann Rothe who filled my life with dreams and gave me wings to reach them.

Flowering Inferno:
Tales of Sinking Hearts

The Word Weaver

To Joan[*] who for centuries ventured through life's oceans believing that he was looking for his own identity when in truth, like Telemachus, he searched for the Ulysses-father-hero that every man wishes for in his youth.

* * *

In the clearing of a dell, they found the house of Circê, well built with shaped stones. Surrounding it were wolves and lions of the mountains, really men whom she had bewitched by giving them poisonous drugs.

Homer

* Joan, Catalan for Juan, John.

He was momentarily blinded by the beautiful mane of her hair that reflected the burst of a thousand reddish lights from the violent shimmer of Houston's summer sunsets. It was as if he had stepped into a magic zone in which time nor senses had any relevance. She was heading toward the classic and modern language building when Rodrigo got a glimpse of her back, enhanced by the brightest aura of a luscious mass of hair, the likes of which he had never seen before. She was singing, or so it seemed to him, with such a melodious voice that, for an instant, his senses were suspended and literally petrified.

"What's up? You look like you've seen a ghost or a creature from beyond the grave," remarked Eva, while the woman with the gorgeous tresses majestically climbed the three stone steps leading to the building.

"Who is she?" asked Rodrigo, pointing at her with a subtle nod of his head.

"Who do ya think? Everybody knows her! She's Professor Thompson, of the Department of classics. Everyone at the U knows her 'cause she's such an eccentric. She's the teacher you were asking me about yesterday, when you registered for her class."

Opening the door of the building, she suddenly turned and fixed her eyes on Rodrigo with a stare of smoldering fire. At that moment, the lights in her hair lost all their splendor. He could hardly believe it when suddenly, superimposed on the divine creature's image, he perceived a grotesque human being. In a sudden transformation, the youth that before had lent magic lights to the sun's rays tangled in her hair, had turned it into the withering fur of a dead rat, oily and dirty. What shocked him the most was that, in spite of the distance that separated them, he instantly absorbed her penetrating and repulsive reek of loneliness, total abandonment, like a place that had never been cleaned. He felt nausea, compassion, fear...

"She's a pitiful sight," Eva added. "She comes to the U looking like a poverty-stricken bag lady who's endured too many failures, you know the kind, the ones who carry a few bottles in a plastic bag, stand in line at Catholic Charities and spend their time rummaging in trash cans. She looks so dirty and disheveled, without make-up. And the hem of her skirt half undone, didn't you see her? That's the way she always comes to class."

Rodrigo solomely added, "She walks without energy, as though she could hardly take another step in life and would rather lose herself in the maze of death."

"No, no," said Eva in a dramatic tone of mockery as she exaggerated theatrical gestures with her hands, "'in the regions of Hades where the blind clairvoyant Tiresias lives,' as Professor Thompson would say. Her mind is pathetically overloaded with stale literature and Greek mythology."

"You're kidding me, Eva! That scarecrow dressed as a beggar can't be a professor, least of all of classics."

"Isn't she a sight? You're in for more, Rodrigo. Just wait till you're in her class!"

And Eva burst out laughing as she headed for the philosophy building. Her last words of warning to watch out for professor Thompson were drowned out by the high-piched clatter of a truck that was picking up garbage.

Rodrigo caught a brief glimpse of Professor Thompson peering at him from behind the sleek glass door, staring at him as though she knew she had been the subject of their conversation. He didn't know if the setting sun's influence on the glass was a false image again, but he knew it was true that he felt mesmerized once more by the bewitching first sight of her. She manifested herself to him in all the splendor of her magnificently abundant and gorgeous hair surrounded by the aura of magic lights that gave her the halo of a goddess emerging from a strange world of fantasy.

From that day on, she continued to appear to Rodrigo in her double personality: as a young bewitching woman and old bag lady. Even during classes he couldn't stop the images from sneaking into his mind. In the beginning, fearing that the effect of the double chimeric obsession might affect his studies, Rodrigo was tempted to drop the course on Homer. Yet a mysterious and uncontrollable force of unknown origin made him stay with it. To justify his inertia, he repeated to himself, with little conviction, that he had substantial reasons to stick it out, the strongest being his curiosity. Yes, curiosity, because in his daily contact with classmates he hoped one of them might reveal experiencing similar strange mirages. However, nobody ever mentioned anything as absurd as what was happening to him. His classmates seemed to bask in jokes about her sloppy appearance, finding no pity in the woman who had reached her limits and lost hope.

Nevertheless, all of them acknowledged that Dr. Thompson was exceptional among her peers, that her classes were fascinating because she vividly brought Ulysses, Patroclus, Nausicaa, Penelope, Telemachus and Achilles to life.

As a matter of fact, when she developed her 'subject it was impossible to remain indifferent to the attraction of that remote world. And it took hold of Rodrigo's mind as something real and factual, that had never died and would never disappear. On several occasions Rodrigo had a strong feeling that instead of just saying words, the teacher was weaving a "divine cloth" (cloth-weave-texture-text) for him, and only him. It was a fragile, graceful and splendid labor of the gods that the "venerable Circe" undertook in her palace, also built by Homer with nothing but words. During classes, caught in the beautiful weft that she wove with words, words, and more words, Rodrigo grew ecstatic, far more happy than when he was dealing with reality. Brief relationships, innocuous conversations, erotic and violent films, the pain of having discovered the infidelities of his domineering father, the painful submission of his sweet, kind, resigned mother, the threatening fierce news that attacked him from newspapers, radio, TV, and even the university's textbooks. The course on Homer was like a perfect paradise to him, where he could avidly drink the cool stream of that river of words that swept away all his sorrows, anxieties and worries, leaving him as clean and powerful as a homeric hero.

Professor Thompson was aware of the magical effect that the warp of her words had on Rodrigo. She never passed up the chance to overwhelm him with words spun to suggest she understood him. She wrote comments at the bottom of his essays and on the translations he turned in to her, sometimes sliping in a secret, clandestine note. At first, the messages focussed on his potential.

> *Rodrigo, in view of what you say and write in class, I realize that you are extremely intelligent, far above most people. It is extraordinary that your sensitivity and intuition allow you to gather sophisticated and multidimensional data that others can't even guess. You are unaware of it, but in your particular case, it is a rare phenomenon that you are able to fully conjugate the creative and innovative power of intuition and the analytical strength of problem solving and reasoning. To think that I had prided myself for being more*

intelligent and qualified than many! (Forgive my arrogance.) Compared to you, I experience the sensation that you have come into my life as one of those mythological heroes that we study and who appear in order to disrupt all current rules of normalcy, eventually to settle triumphantly in the center of the world. What I tell you is a truth that you must accept and feel proud of, as I feel, because together we are a couple separated from the rest of humanity. Please, don't try —it would be useless— to escape from such destiny, as you have been trying to extricate yourself since I first met you.

Rodrigo was amazed at such an analysis, which revealed a strong interest in him. Besides, it seemed the professor interpreted the "destiny," stuck in the middle of the page, in the rigid and inevitable Greek meaning. She was warning him about the contents of the oracle by means of her assumed witchcraft powers. To further complicate matters, in a letter attached to his essay on Ulysses' descent into Hades, she wove more words.

Because you are exactly as I previously analyzed it is very difficult for you to find a simple answer to your obsessive quest to find who you are. Don't forget that any satisfactory answer shall always be highly complex. Remember that existentialism proclaims: everyone is what he chooses to be. Ulysses decided to be a hero. You waver between the unlimited ventures of Ulysses and the few present demands of young Rodrigo, caught in the superfluous trappings of the family's bourgeois life style, which does not suit him in the least. If I were in your place, I would be indignant at the unfairness of your family which even deprives its members of freedom by subjecting them to frivolous rules and demands. No matter how limited the freedom of a human being may be, we all have the unavoidable duty to defend it if we don't want to be alienated.

In a Helter-skelter sort of way, she continued to send him messages. In one of them, she mentioned the *"desperate need"* that he had to establish a healthy and intimate relationship with someone. Strangely enough, Rodrigo never alluded to this or anything else that she said, although he reluctantly acknowledged that there was quite some truth to her speculations. It was obvious that the woman had magic powers, either that, or she mastered psychology. Among other things, she told him that she felt sorry for him, so helpless to defend himself from his family's impositions and accept what was so important to him, an intimate relationship with someone. She added that it broke her heart to witness this because inevitably he had to fulfill his destiny (destiny again!) and so break the ties that subjected him to the petty-bourgeois philosophy of his family. With this note, in a separate envelope, and to Rodrigo's great surprise, she sent him a key to her home and a map, which at the bottom she wrote:

> *This is the map, dear boy, that will take you through the labyrinths of Houston's highways to my home, the refuge that will save you from existential death, imposed upon you by those who say they love you when in fact they are destroying you.*

From then on, Professor Thompson never missed a chance to send him all kinds of messages. In them, she aptly analyzed Rodrigo's idiosyncracies, the intensity of his problems and emotions and his exacerbated sensitivity misunderstood by most who called him neurotic or psychopathic, often applying labels used to qualify any misunderstood behavior beyond the reaches of common intelligence. In another letter she wrote:

> *I am not at all afraid of the intensity of your emotions and outbursts, and therefore I promise never to abandon you. You must know, dearest Rodrigo, that to me you may also reveal the whole threatening spectrum of your thoughts, anger and emotions. I understand you and accept the depth of your frustrations. To me you may also expose all that you have repressed for fear of being misunderstood.*
>
> *You have more than enough reasons to believe that what you see, perceive, think and feel is wrong. Nevertheless, none of it is wrong, only different from what others see, perceive, think, and feel. You must trust yourself more, Rodrigo, my dear boy. You must realize that my duty toward you is to communicate, infuse, and saturate you with confidence in*

your talents and the extent of your potential. My other task on your behalf is to free you from your family and the demanding social obligations they impose on you. I promise to cut the ties that bind your hands once and for all because they keep you from giving yourself to me. This latter task requires that both of us enjoy private hours and that you come to see me when the pressures of the external world hurt you, so you can share your frustrations and sorrows with me. You don't want to acknowledge it, but since the first day I saw you through the glass door of the language building, I perceived in your eyes an intense death wish, a desire to end your precious life forever. Since then, my love for you has constantly intensified, and because I love you, Rodrigo, because you have become my whole world, I shall fight with all my strength and devote my whole life to save you from yourself.

Upon reading it, Rodrigo experienced a strange void in his soul and instant shame, rejection, anger and contempt toward the old bag lady-trash-can-rummager. Nevertheless, the intense aroma of loneliness that emanated from her (through a senseless and strange association) reminded him of his frail mother's loneliness, always humiliated by the youthful brilliance of his father's mistresses. Then, he failed to follow through on his decision to leave Homer's class. Likewise, his determination to confront Professor Thompson and scream at her to face the truth, look at herself in a mirror and consider that her fiftyish appearance, her face already furrowed by wrinkles and her total lack of beauty made a mockery of her ludicrous efforts to seduce a young man his age. But upon facing her, Rodrigo lowered his eyes and became overwhelmed by the deeply established social code of refinement-hipocracy-pretense, which surfaced with a yes, Dr. Thompson, how can I help you? Let me carry your satchel made so heavy by books, allow me to open the door, don't worry, you know I'm here to serve you, just tell me what you want, order whatever you wish from me. So it was after one of her classes, with the pretext that frequent muggings and rapes in the Montrose area threatened her safety, she asked Rodrigo escort her to her car.

"Where are you parked, Rodrigo?" Professor Thompson asked once she was already in her car with her foot on the accelerator.

"Just a few blocks from here because today I had a lot of trouble finding a parking space nearby. There must be a concert or lecture which explains why it's so crowded around here."

"I'll take you there. Get in."

With trepidation and deep reluctance Rodrigo stepped into the old, shabby Chevrolet with the gun-smoke metal patches left unpainted after old dents were hammered out of the sides by a body shop. The cracked dashboard and torn vinyl seats whizzed out stale-smelling air each time he moved slightly. His legs started to shake when he vividly remembered one of her letters detailing that in order for her to defend him from the death (the Hades!) that pervaded his whole being, he must abandon everything, absolutely everything, and come to live with her in her mansion. Yes, she used the word mansion, which struck him as odd that a woman with her sloppy appearance would refer to her house as a mansion. It was in Sugarland, where only her cats could rob her of a little time while she devoted the bulk of it to him. In her mansion she would cater to all his needs and wishes:

> *I'll take you to my paradise, Rodrigo, to give you the peace and quiet you need, with no presence other than that of my legion of cats. You may give my telephone number to your relatives and friends so you don't cut contact with them. You will see that there, with me, we shall reach the utmost peace and happiness, because you know that I love you with the most solid and total of loves, like no one, not even your mother, has ever loved you.*

Rodrigo had no doubt that she was a superb manipulator of words, words that she wove like a tight web in which he gradually and unavoidably felt caught, just as he did at that moment in the car. No sooner did he sink into the springless vinyl car seat, that the penetrating odor of cats' urine and excrement provoked him to become uncontrollably nauseated. Professor Thompson had left two of her cats in the car while she dictated four hours of classes and now they glared at him with anger and resentment. Then, in the car's dingy darkness, he caught the golden glimmer of a feline glare. Or was it pity that the golden fire of their eyes conveyed to him? There was such a human quality in their pupils!

Then, amid the twilight that invaded the ludicrous, shabby Chevrolet, once again she appeared to Rodrigo in the full splendor of the youthful red haired beauty of their first encounter. Suddenly, Rodrigo felt a strong, depressing conviction that there was nothing he could do to defend himself from her, he was truly, irrevocably caught in her web of words, words and more words. Oral, written, whispered, spoken, read, recited words. But please, no, I want to go home, let me go, it's getting late, my parents expect me for dinner. Don't be foolish, my beloved boy, they only impose duties on you while I will give you the capacity to forget. Complete oblivion of everything: pain, duties, demands, repressions. Watch now. See how the invisible vapors of this atomizer eliminate the pungent smell of cats in this car? That's how your past will disappear instantly. You will enter my mansion, forbidden to all others. From now on, just you and I, you and I, will share my paradise. Only you and I. The external world eliminated forever.

* * *

"Are you aware, Dr. Thompson, that since last Thursday, after your class, Rodrigo Carrillo has been missing from his home and has never telephoned his family?" Claudia, one of the students in the class, asked.

"Oh! I didn't know!"

"Since only recently Mark Kilroy was a helpless victim of the macabre butchery, I mean, the satanic sacrifice in Matamoros. The Carrillo family and the police are looking for Rodrigo, afraid that he might be another victim of the drug dealers."

"The newspapers claim the worst is feared, and to make things worse, there isn't the slightest clue to follow," Hector, Rodrigo's closest friend, commented with obvious anxiety. "They only know what we've told them, that he attended class on Thursday and afterward didn't even pick up his convertible. It was found parked in the same place where he left it at noon, when we returned from a snack. Since the day before yesterday another gang of drug dealers who also practice satanic rituals was discovered in this neighborhood, so you can imagine his family's anxiety."

"Didn't the cops interrogate you as they did us?"

"Oh! Yes, yes, but what could I tell them? Rodrigo must be visiting some of his relatives in Miami, those he speaks about so often.

I have a hunch that wherever he is, he's not in danger... no danger at all. Let us continue with Homer. We were discussing the paragraph in which Ulysses and his comrades arrive at the island of Eea."

Hector fixed his eyes on the page with the description of how those who left the ship and entered the house "heard the beautiful goddess within singing in a lovely voice, as she worked at the web on her loom, a large web of incorruptible stuff, a glorious thing of delicate gossamer fabric, such as goddesses make." When he looked up at Professor Thompson he could hardly believe his eyes. Instead of the tall, strong, fat, sloppy woman on the verge of old age holding a hard and bitter expression on her face, an incredible transformation had taken place before him. Was he dreaming? He was now looking at a young, beautiful and attractive woman with a shock of reddish hair, a golden aura that gave her the appearance of a powerful goddess. And, instead of the loud, shrieking voice he was used to hearing, she was describing in a melodious tone what he perceived as a divine chant, how Ulysses' comrades were turned into pigs by Circê: "for they now had pigs' heads and grunts and bristles, pigs all over except that their minds were the same as before. There they were then, miserably shut up in the pigsty."

The Secret World of Grandma Anacleta

Today is a day which we never had before, which we shall never have again. It rose from the great ocean of eternity, and again sinks into its unfathomable depths.

Thomas De Witt Talmadge

In the oceanic vastness of the baroque bed framed by richly carved twisting columns, under the sheets and the ballooning eider-down, the minimal body of grandma Anacleta had withered and reduced to naught after nine decades. From the vantage point of my ten years, probably for lack of a larger perspective, Grandma Anacleta was nothing but a small pile of bones and wrinkled skin. She spent motionless hours only moving her lips incessantly as though talking to herself. In spite of all our efforts, none of us had been able to make sense of the endless muttering that emanated from her lips. In the beginning, with the patience of Job, we tried to establish a closeness, to the point that we became constantly attentive to her incessant mumblings. Little by little, we gave up and the time came when she was so insignificant to us that we paid more attention to the television, radio and even the lawn mower. To make up for our indifference and avoid feeling guilty, we bought her a Walkman that only she could hear through the headset placed on her ears. That blessed modern contraption performed the miraculous miracle of stopping Grandma Anacleta's mutterings and forever dissipated the threatening clouds of guilt from us! From then on we only paid attention to her when she cared to join our daily reality and fill the house with her loud, broken voice. Even now, her distant memory brings back my amazement at the incredible strength contained in that small pile of skin and bones which could shake the glass of water she always left on her night table. We all trembled when her broken voice burst out screaming: "somebody bring me my bed pan right now! Water, a glass of water with ice! Tell Norma to come and fix my sheets. Why doesn't anyone come? Am I a picture on the wall?" Who knows how many impertinent demands she uttered, like a captain leading soldiers, making her presence a powerful ruler of the house, a million times stronger and bigger than she actually was.

Her cracking voice surged from the huge baroque bed like a powerful missile directed skillfully to each one of us. The projectile pierced my body and I felt remorse down to the marrow of my consciousness, stirring at the question of whether my duty might be to forever lament the tragedy of that body thrown like a useless rag on the bed, a body that only recovered its soul to utter despotic commands.

For Mom, the loud cracked voice of Grandma Anacleta meant an indefinite sentence to stay by her side and read to her. At the beginning it was only the Bible. Later, to our bewildererment, she demanded not just the classics but also contemporary writers. Yet, they had to be substantial, otherwise she'd grab the book from Mom's hands and throw it against the wall.

"These shitty writers mock us by feeding us verbosity with the sole intent of hiding their stupidity! Trash, chaff, rubbish! As Unamuno said."

The truth is that Grandma Anacleta knew what she wanted from books, and poor Mom, although she liked books and their reviews, was constantly fearful because at the slightest provocation the tyrannical voice might emerge from the bed uttering curses against the author, some of their characters, and even against Mom who in the course of reading might have fallen asleep from exhaustion.

"It seems unbelievable that you can be so tired at your age. Learn from me! Although I'm almost a century old, I feel fully alive! People today are nothing but little bits of shit wrapped in tissue paper because they truly lack spirit," shouted Grandma. Mom never even thought of protesting because Grandma Anacleta didn't pay attention to anybody, much less her own daughter.

For Norma, the Samaritan granddaughter, Grandma's imperious voice was a force that set her immediately into efficient motion, propelling her toward the pile of bones and corrugated skin that formed the bed, uttering machine-gun-likc orders: bring me the bed pan, take away the washbowl and the towel, you already cleaned me properly, don't be a fool, girl, and straighten up my damn bed, my sole refuge and kingdom all day through... because I'm old and shriveled they believe I'm a nuisance, good for nothing, but they are wrong! Tomorrow I'll be ninety years old and I represent the voice of wisdom and experience.

We believed it. Even Dad did, because usually before an event would take place, she'd always predict it as a clairvoyant and warn us. She predicted the disastrous marriage of Anselma to Rogelio, the fortune hunter who scarcely knows what to do except watch the grass grow all day. She also predicted the failure of Dad's business, and everything turned out exactly the way she said it would.

In short, Grandma Anacleta was just a little pile of flesh and bones with a voice of thunder that shook the house and its inhabitants, and a clear, farsighted mind whenever she felt like meddling in our affairs. Nevertheless, if she didn't want to talk, we'd beg her to speak up but she'd only answer with her stubborn silence. So we always tolerated her and loved her in spite of her quirks. Oh! I almost forgot, she kept up to date on current events to the last detail. It pleased her so to talk about Gorbachev as though he were a neighbor, and she went as far as to say that she was becoming a lover of Russia, short of adding that she was a Marxist, always expounding angrily against the wastes of capitalism while she passionately defended the proletariat adopting the role of its number one counsel. She commented in detail about the destruction of the rain forests in Brazil, the hunger in Africa and the Panama Canal and its history. And she kept up with the number of goals made by Maradona, Pele, and God knows how many other famous soccer stars. Once Grandma told me that according to Virginia Woolf, a woman needed two things to write novels and short stories: money and a room of her own. "But this is an impossible ambition because men continue being our lords and masters and will always deprive us of both rights!," was her grievous and often repeated litany. "Have you noticed that there are practically no female composers in the world of music? Music makes itself felt by sound, whereas the female writer's pen silently runs over her paper as she secretly, as if committing a sin, defies men with her books."

We knew that the Walkman, whose headset she always held close to her ears, like leaches, was the rich source of her knowledge because she never asked for a newspaper or watched television.

On her birthday, Marcos had the idea of giving her a couple of bowling balls, black and shiny as the floor of the vestibule that the maid Chelita kept mopping with as much success as Sisyphus. Uproariously amused by the joke and speculation of Grandma Anacleta's surprise upon seeing the balls, we placed them in a box and wrapped it in beautiful pink paper suitable for a newborn baby, and then we crowned it with a huge matching bow.

"Now, be careful, Sonia, don't stand near Grandma Anacleta because in a fit of temper the strength in her voice may slip to her hand. Whoosh! She might throw the bowling balls in your direction and knock you out in a single blow. Don't forget, you've gotta protect yourself from getting hurt." Marcos warned me with the protective air of an older brother. I thanked him, deeply touched by his thoughtfulness, because to see Grandma better I used to climb onto her bed or the frame of the mattress.

"Can you imagine, Marcos, being so frail and skinny, those bowling balls would squash me. A cockroach could survive better."

The irrepressible force of our defiant laughter was such that we could hardly finish tying the bow on the gift box. Her birthday was actually the next day, and until then, every passing hour we joyfully anticipated the effects of our mischief.

However, to our amazement, those two bony arms covered by parched dry skin grabbed the balls as though they were weightless. Marcos and I looked at each other stunned, asking ourselves if, by mistake, instead of the balls we might have placed some light objects in the box. Yet, we had no doubt and knew for certain what was inside. Our initial surprise was followed by another when after we positioned ourselves safely out of reach from her angry object-throwing reaction, she opened the package and her face lit up as though she were looking at the Holy Grail and our gift had terminated an endless quest.

"Aha! this, precisely this, is what I wanted. How did you guess? I never mentioned what I wanted. When I was young, well, let's say in my forties, this was my favorite sport. I was among the best!"

After the bowling balls incident, Mom was free from the slavish task of reading by the huge baroque bed. Nevertheless, once in a while she stopped by Grandma's room to ask if she wanted her to read her something. The answer was always drastic.

"Damn, all to hell! Haven't I told you already that I don't want it? The time for action has arrived. ACTION, just as you hear it... underlined."

We all looked at each other asking ourselves what she meant by "the time for action" and the truth is that none of us could figure it out. Until one sunny orange blossom redolent morning, her voice firmly and clearly resounded in the house with the ringing of resurrection.

"Norma, bring me my black slacks and sweater with the red blouse, my going out clothes."

Going out clothes? Which? For twenty years she had stayed secluded in the ample baroque bed without ever leaving it, not even for her most elementary needs. Not one of us failed to fear that this was the obvious sign that preceded her departure from this world, well dressed so as to save us the trouble of shrouding her.

"And may we ask where you want to go, Grandma Anacleta?" asked Norma, stuttering from fear that she might answer that she was stepping into the other world.

It wasn't so and she only said, "Stop asking, you fool! Wash me quickly because I want to leave right away."

We couldn't believe our ears! She jumped lightly out of the big ornate bed and dressed without any help. We all realized then that this apparently frail woman had lived all those years torturing us and turning us into her slaves with the only purpose of holding us under her control. To display such agility and carry out her well premeditated plan, she certainly had to have rehearsed and exercised for many years. Just then, we found the explanation for the sounds of steps and movements that came from her bedroom late at night, when there was only silence and quiet in the rest of the house. We even thought that a ghost was roaming in her room and we called Father Baltasar to perform an exorcism. Now we knew why Grandma laughed uproariously under the sheets while the priest sprinkled the wall and furniture with holy water and read latin psalms.

"Where is the bowling alley? Marcos, take me to the bowling alley in your Volkswagen."

"But Grandma Anacleta...what are you going to do at the bowling alley?"

"Are you really stupid or just pretending? Why would anyone go to the bowling alley if not to play, you damned fool? Didn't you and your sister give me some bowling balls for my ninetieth birthday? Why would I, Anacleta Gutierrez del Castillo, leave them in a storeroom when it's the best present I have received in my life? I'd have to be crazy! Come on, young man, let's get to the bowling alley. You'll see your Grandma win the world championship and the media will broadcast the most wonderful message to the world. It's necessary to fill the earth with marvels in order to empty it of so much brutality and corruption around us! Besides, this would be a double triumph since I'm a woman and very old. Can you imagine the newspaper headlines announcing the feat? "NINETY-YEAR-OLD GRANDMOTHER WORLD BOWLING CHAMPION?"

History's Editor

The smile that you send out returns to you.
Indian wisdom.

The neighbor's old and dilapidated pick-up truck always parked in front of the North windows of her house day after day in the course of years gradually became her sole companion in her daily barren, useless existence. When she opened the North windows she felt overwhelmed by mixed feelings of tenderness, gratitude and relief. As long as the pick-up truck was there, it was obvious that somebody continued to live in the crumbling house across the street. That "somebody," a solitary man, puny, and melancholy like herself, spent many long hours inside his house. Only once in a while would he leave on an errand, returning soon to quickly disappear within the walls of his home.

She anxiously followed every movement he made, his comings and goings, which after all were also the comings and goings of the pick-up truck. She, who loudly complained of the twentieth century materialism, even started to feel shame for her dependency on such a dilapidated object, which actually was just one of the many gadgets of this mechanized age.

"Why feel embarrassed considering the pick-up truck is only the symbol of a presence that obliterates the emptiness and the undeserved absence of all company? It's a possible refuge to which I may turn when I need someone in my old age, plagued by senility, decrepitude, neglect and loneliness. But that dried-up man with his flesh-rid features is inaccessible. I don't even know his name. Only once in a while over a good-morning, hello, good-bye, I agonize over the conviction that my only hope of comfort relies on the pick-up truck's presence, on him, his ins and outs-pacing-walks-absences-returns. At night the light from his windows calms my anxiety but it is mostly the dilapidated body of the vehicle. To have it facing me, sometimes like a protective shadow in the darkness of my life, is all things to me — my salvation —guarantee of my endurance, that a short distance from my home's walls other walls rise to shelter another being who breathes and exists like myself..."

Old age is bitter because after giving birth and strength to Nacha and Joaquin and encouraging them to follow the distant highways of profession and marriage, they only manifested themselves through birthday and Christmas cards. They turned into voices slithering along the fine telephone wires with a "hello, mother, how are you?" "Good, very good," "I got a promotion. Pepito now has his first tooth. Anita is at the top of her class. The project I submitted to the company won an award. No, we can't visit for Christmas because I have to work. The corporation assigned my colleague to a job in Europe. So we shall leave the children with my mother-in-law and we will travel with him, sorry, mom, we hope you have a nice Christmas and New Year. We're sure your friends will keep you company and you'll have a great time. Sure, we'll be having lots of fun and your Holidays will also be very happy. Bye. Adriana and your grandchildren send their love."

She hangs up the telephone feeling a great emptiness invade every visceral cavity in her body. But soon afterward experiences a tide of grateful tenderness looking at the pick-up truck across the street, her only companion and daily comfort. If the children leave us, if nothing lasts in life and everything fades and disappears, the pick-up truck carries with it the threat that one day it might not be across the street from her home, that her neighbor might move away and take the truck with him forever. Fear. Horror. Anxiety... and the impulse to run and knock on the neighbor's door (what is his name?) and talk to him.

"Listen to me, whatever your name is, I'm here to tell you that you, your pick-up truck and the faint lights in some of your windows keep me more precious company than my children's cards and voices on the telephone, and I ask myself, if you are alone and I'm also alone, why can't we be friends, even if we only talk about the weather, our children's selfishness, the high cost of living, the marvelous political changes in the Soviet Union, the withdrawal of troops from Afghanistan, or that the leaves are already falling, and that another year went by so fast, or the famine in Africa, or the many dead in the Armenian earthquake...? We could find so much to talk about! Enough to fill the slow hours of each day with words, words, words that offer company, obliterate loneliness, cancel the silence that precedes the eternal silence of the grave."

Ah! But in this Anglo-Saxon society I have no right to seek such company. Here, Hispanics are considered hysteric-mediocre-half starved nobodies with no claim to or merit to reach the glorious American dream of owning a home, Mercedes-Benz, furs, jewels, art objects, and so on, our Hispanic weakness falls apart in competition with the cement, iron and metal of the "gringo" colossus. My neighbor (I wonder what his name is) would open his door and look at me from the blond height of his racial pride and I would feel like a human cockroach with no other right than to continue hiding my loneliness behind the brick walls of my home, where I must always refrain my fear of rapists that walk through the city streets with death rotting in their hands; hiding my fear of the daily heavy silence, and the terror of knowing that my only company is the pick-up truck, and the voices and music from my stereo, seldom a familiar voice on the telephone, because when I try to reach someone another machine answers me. More and more gadgets and automated monstrosities impede dialogue among humans. Mirringa is the only one who sustains an elementary communication with me. Her meows and the mysterious millinery depth in her iridescent gaze tells me that she knows my most intimate secrets as though I had confided in her; the sinuous, sensual movements of her supple body give me the only measure of affection and communication... Is there a deeper loneliness than mine? What would happen if the pick-up truck was never again parked across the street?

* * *

Spring brought with it vacation time so she left to spend several weeks with her two grandchildren, Nacha's sons, on the beaches of Padre Island, a well-deserved retribution for the courage she displayed in facing the empty monotony of her life.

At the vacation's end, she returned determined to establish contact with her neighbor, once and for all. It didn't matter at all if he misinterpreted her actions because of her Hispanic origin. When one lives in a situation on the edge of despair, nothing matters very much. A drowning man grabs even the most fragile floating object to stay alive. So why shouldn't she show up at his door with one of those finger-licking pecan pies she used to bake? And do you know... Mr.? Mr. what? Alright, so Mr. Whoever-You-Are, do you know what your pick-up truck means to me? Yes, that's what I said: your pick-up truck parked facing my kitchen window, looks to me like a monument to solidarity, companionship, friendship, dialogue... Your pick-up truck is hope incarnate... More still, a whole sheaf of hopes... there is such an understanding between us that I'm deeply moved when I see it, no, don't think I'm crazy, your pick-up truck gives me a feeling of security, I feel safe, protected. As long as it is there in plain view I don't feel so lonesome because we have created a secret pact... But when I don't see it, I'm distressed! Anxious! Restless! I keep coming and going aimlessly through the house, frightened by any small rustling that may suggest the presence of rapists, thieves, murderers, who knows which? More than anything I fear my heart's echoes pounding wildly through the empty landscape of my loneliness. Do you know now how much your pick-up truck means to me? It reveals your presence nearby, the possibility of now and then detecting a light in a window at night, or the raising of a blind during the day. The sound of the truck's motor starting before the truck takes you somewhere or upon your return, the anxiously expected purring of the engine when it stops under my kitchen window, is the most beautiful, triumphant hymn of glory and peace. For me, heaven's angels couldn't perform a chorus to give me such intense feelings of delight, which makes me ask myself, with a painful knot in my throat, what would happen to me if you and your pick-up truck were to disappear forever from that comforting place in my daily life?

Her firm decision became paralyzed in her soul when from a distance she saw her neighbor's home but no pick-up truck. Instead, many cars were parked along the curb and people were coming and going from the house. Was he having a party? Had he parked the pick-up truck elsewhere to make room for his guests' cars? It had been a long time since he had a party... Yes, in the past he did once in a while. Yes, he did.

As she approached her home, she realized that there was no party. Instead, a mournful mood seemed to pervade the atmosphere which she had already sensed with a bitter premonition. Even before getting her suitcases into the house, with impulsive rashness, her heart pounding in her throat, she stopped the first persons that crossed her path and addressed him with a voice made thin by fear.

"Mr. Hamilton hung himself. He was found yesterday," was the answer to her question. "Are you his neighbor?"

"Mr. Hamilton?" (So, Hamilton was his name. *Was*, because now he's dead and our projected dialogue will be buried with him).

"Are you his neighbor?"

She nodded in affirmation, unable to utter a single word, and she remained motionless while the man continued to explain.

"A long message for you was found in one of the deceased's pockets. You may speak with his former wife who is in the house today receiving condolences and trying to put some order in the chaos he left behind. She can give you details about the contents of the note because to him, you... I assume it is you since he refers to the neighbor across the street who, like him, lives alone, while other neighbors have their families with them. I mean that to him you were his only company, well, it's absurd to talk about company in this context because Mr. Hamilton seems to have been guessing, hour after hour, about your presence in your own home. At night he looked for a light in the frame of a window, the blinds you raised in the morning and pulled down in the evening, your voice when you called your cat. Mirringa? Isn't that her name? Mirringa?" She nodded again while crying silently.

"Most of all, in the note he insists on what it meant to him to see your car parked by your garage....Yet, strangely, he never mentions that there was a friendship between you two, or anything of the kind. I can assure you that it is a very intriguing note, because he insists that your Toyota, Ma'am, was for him... Yes, if I remember correctly, he says that it represented a monument to solidarity, companionship, friendship and dialogue for him... hope, how would I know? He ends the note by saying that your long, endless absence made him realize that he would never again enjoy your distant presence neither would he see your Toyota, and that loneliness and emptiness, his sole companions in the future, had closed in on him like a dark night penetrating to the marrow of his soul, and to that point he couldn't stand it anymore. He gave up and decided, once and for all, to put an end to the suffocating hell of a hopeless desolation.

The Burden of Routine

There are things that happen in the dark between a man and a woman.

Tennessee Williams

The door closed behind him. She, the bride who only yesterday had pinned orange blossoms on her veil, dressed in white and emotionally pronounced a "yes" full of joy and as far-reaching as the whole wide world, jumped hurriedly from the nuptial bed and started to dig frantically into the recesses of her deepest memories. She was horrified that after enduring the humiliating and painful experience of her wedding night, a degrading metamorphoses — she couldn't recall the memory of her wedding ceremony. Her memories had ceased. Mixed in with the scraps and crumbs he had left after slaughtering her feelings, she could hardly bring back into focus the rose bud he had placed in her hair on a distant evening filled with music and sweet loving chatter. The poetry which in the failing light of sunset took the shape of a heart in love, now seemed like an unrecognizable and bitter omen of murky presage. She also recalled, in the midst of such destruction, the small music box, still playing distant melodies that her fiance had given her with "Stardust" as a theme. Kisses, caresses, and walks through the woods, promises, laughter, dreams for the future, everything that led her to pronounce the "yes", the most important "yes" in her life, was now at the very bottom of her trash-can-memory, smothered by the wedding night, when with his proud macho arrogance and without concern he discarded the pitiful bloodied shreds of her deepest feelings.

Considering such carnage, bewildered, on the verge of terror, repressing the nausea that cramped not her stomach but the deepest abyss of her being, she continued to extract more and more ghastly shreds from the bottom of her memory. With utter disappointment, she realized that the promises of eternal-paradise-my-dearest-love-of-my-life, had turned into a nest of vipers. That evening he reached the root of her mercilessly torn virginity, that evening so full of distress, she reached the conviction that she had taken a definite and irreversible step toward hell.

She had no other way out but through suicide. Nevertheless, when at the end of the day he turned the key of the front door and said "hello, my dear, what did you do today?" she rummaged among the most generous and self-sacrificing traits of her being and came up with a smile, kissed him on the lips and exclaimed, "It was a beautiful, wonderful day!"

Thus, she courageously placed herself under the yoke of routine and enslavement that marriage is supposed to be, just as she had seen other women do, starting with grandmother and then mother, as well as sisters, relatives, friends, neighbors, and unknown women, all of them. Now she was under the yoke just the same.

Future Sorrows

To my dear friend Hugo Lindo, Central America's master of the short story, in grateful remembrance.

***

Who can predict everything? Who is able to warn of future sorrows?

Thomas de Kempis

In her most absurd dreams — since her childhood she allowed herself to engage in fantastic daydreams to compensate for the daily drudgery of reality — she had never before conceived anything so extraordinary. She couldn't dispel her amazement. The minute Mr. Congos, representative of TWD Business Systems Inc., came into her own home, she had trouble comprehending the exotic coupling of science, technology, mechanics, imagination, art and mystery taking place. Right under her own roof! How did it happen? In the typewriter, word processor, computer, word cruncher, whatever you call it.

Who knows what this marvelous machine is now called! In these rushed times everything changes shape, name and function while constantly progressing ad infinitum. God knows why the names that before their inception about four decades ago, names which clung to objects and remained closely attached to them, now change in the blink of an eye, as easily as one changes into another suit. I may be getting old very fast and that's why I resist change, like my parents and my grandparents before them. Still things continue to evolve like the typewriters. We must accept this. It's progress. But acceptance highlights my defeat. Life's a miracle that to me seems increasingly baffling. What a dismal joke! Only a few days ago the fortieth anniversary of the invasion of Normandy was celebrated... "D-Day" ... And on that same Tuesday another portent occurred: the word processor that is the convergency of such different, irreconcilable words came into my home. Who could have guessed it!

When Mr. Congos brought the computer in, I thought

How very odd! Today not even bread or milk are delivered to homes, and this has gone on for years. Ah! but a computer just out of the factory, smelling new, redolent of office, stationery and ink; yes, they bring it in and place it on the desk as if it were fine porcelain. But enough digressing. It's obvious that the blasted machine makes me ramble...

So, I repeat, when Mr. Congos delivered the processor, he demonstrated how to use all the numerous and complex buttons that can't be rightfully called keys anymore.

Then he explained, "in the last twenty years, this contraption has reached the utmost efficiency in electronic technology due to its high precision and unlimited amount of programs it can process." Yeah, that's what every salesman says about the product he sells.

Her enthusiasm was boundless when she found out she'd never again have to write on notebooks with her minuscule handwriting because all the subjects of her stories and novels would be stored in the monumental memory of the word processor. Besides, at that time she tired easily and was prone to forget what she was creating with her imagination. It was definitely a relief to know she could rely on an almighty memory.

Learning how to operate it was hard, but later it all became so easy and seemed incredible that her magical stories were printed on a television screen and she had the power to correct, edit, change, polish, add, delete, move a paragraph automatically from one place to another, without the risk of losing anything. How could she ever have lived sharpening pencils and scribbling endlessly on sheets of paper? Either that, or using a traditional typewriter to copy some of the pages and shuffle them around until the story or novel was to her liking. And the poor writers of long ago, what an ordeal it must have been to bequeath us their immortal works!

In the electronic monster, she finished filing a story she had been working on for a week: "Future Sorrows."

> *How strange! I always find my titles at the end of my writing. This will be the first empty title that I will have to fill little by little with its content. I have trouble finding suggestive titles. I shuffle, shuffle and shuffle words and more words in a sterile quest. This is the first time. There's always a first time, eh? The other stories turned out very well: "Sinners Crop," "Beyond the Flesh," all of them... What do I know! All of them are now filed in the abyss of that mechanized memory. Now I must provide "Future Sorrows" with a punch line fully deserving of what I've already written. The truth is that I don't know how to finish it... because I can't break years of ritual habit: to feel the pulse of what I've written I need to see it on a page, I must smell the paper, the ink or graphite, see in black and white what I create. To me, the computer's screen looks like a ghostly wall that rises between me and my creation. It seems that what is written on the screen doesn't belong to me. As I progress from one line to the next, it all gradually becomes stranger to me. I'll print it and then see*

what this powerful memory gadget will vomit. What if it didn't record everything I typed as my imagination raced?

She was initially shocked when she typed her own name to locate the file of her stories in the depths of the electronic memory. On the screen, one line below, the following sentence appeared in bold, upper case letters: **RITA CRESO HAS NOT BEEN CREATED YET.** Frightened, she anxiously touched her body with the sudden sensation of finding herself thrown into the most brutal void. She quickly overcame the vertigo and even laughed at her ludicrous stupidity.

A mistake of mechanization, that's all. The machine hasn't yet digested my pen name.

She then searched the MENU and among all the options offered by the computer's screen she chose number **4 - PRINT THE TEXT**. Instantly, the electronic monster started to drum out words at a speed that the most expert typist couldn't match. The irresistible magic of mechanization. To be able to sit still while the computer, by its own accord, rushed on reproducing the full wealth of the imagination's world without a hitch!

Finding herself in that pregnant process of creation, she opted to digress, look through her studio window, watch the autumn leaves fall just as her own years slipped by silently, slowly, in the intense loneliness of her life. Five children had already left her, some to distant universities, others to try their wings, all of them in their own world... like herself. And the big house, in old times full of laughter, voices, screams, weeping, nannies, songs, doors slamming... how lonely, how empty, how hollow it had become... like herself! Then crimes increased like rain showers in October.

"When I woke up and saw that man leaning over my bed, staring at me, I though it was a nightmare, but it was real. He told me to keep quiet if I wanted to stay alive, and then he raped me, I don't know how many times..." Mrs. Reyes' words in the doctor's office yesterday obsessed her, wouldn't leave her alone.

Today nobody is safe, not even at home. Six convicts have escaped from the Warren county prison. Dangerous. One of them was to be executed in August... but now he's free. Did I tightly close the studio door to the yard? Silly, I even turned the double lock! What should I be afraid of? Only my loneliness as a lone old woman steeped in soliloquies and fantasies...

Again she walked toward the door to the courtyard and made sure for the tenth time that it was securely closed with double locks in place. She thought about the irony of her name: Creso, the wealthiest man alive centuries ago, and she, Rita, earned a couple of dollars as a writer. Without her husband's monthly salary, she might not even survive to tell her story.

Meanwhile, the electronic monster finished typing the six pages of "Future Sorrows." Rita Creso quickly started to review the task performed by such an impressive memory. This line could be eliminated. I should find a synonym for "intruder" here. Ah! This hackneyed term about the children "trying their wings" must be changed for something more striking. And the sentence about the woman looking "at the leaves that fall like her own years" is a cliché used time and time again. It should be eliminated.

But there is a minimum of errors. I will correct them in the twinkle of an eye and that's it. It's one of my best stories. I could almost attest, with no exaggeration, that after writing for a lifetime, scribbling on masses of paper, I have finally reached this precise and genial moment in my literary career, as though in these particular lines and words my destiny as a writer had finally been fulfilled. Utter nonsense! Why do we all feel the same? The last thing we write, because it's so close to our present and ourselves, is always the best. But... what's happening? I didn't feed this... this into the memory of the computer... Did it get mixed up with another story? It's my fault that such a whopping mistake has occurred by trusting a machine that, no sooner set in operation, blows a screw and... bang! Good-by accuracy. No, the mix up with other stories must be discarded. I never wrote any of this... not even the style is mine. I'm facing chaos.

Then she remembered the last letter of her friend the poet Jose Jurado Morales who, aware of her enthusiasm with the just-acquired electronic machine, warned her: "Beware of computers! Don't let them go to your head, as it happens with some poets who used them to mechanize their poems!"

> *And now, how can I remember what I filed in that stupid mechanical memory? Now I realize that I never finished the story, yet on the screen I see a horrific blood and death ending, I who always seek an aesthetic cosmovision's logic of harmony and balance! Yet no it's not chaotic. The story follows with impressive accuracy until it reaches the climatic end.*

Overcome by panic, Rita Creso rises from her chair and steps back without taking her eyes off the electronic monster. She suspects, is almost certain, that after having stored several stories in its memory, the infamous artifact has mastered the mechanics of her imagination, the structural process of narrative sequences, the descriptive grammar —as it's called by some modern experts— and even the logic of the language. Resenting its long life of submission to alien dictates, today it writes its version of the story that only Rita Creso has the right to offer her readers. Frightened beyond reason, she realizes that the machine has usurped her role as a writer. Excited and furious, she unplugs it. But instead of going dark immediately, the computer's tiny green square eye blinks slowly and leisurely. Then its whole beastly metallic black body stirs, as though reluctant to stop the throbbing of its electronic circuits, and inexplicably emits a vital sound; one might say as a protest. Rita Creso enters a dense mystery zone. Bewildered, she reads the ending of "Future Sorrows" again to confirm that the electronic monster really printed such a horrendous ending and tried to usurp—did it only try? Has it actually taken over— her personality as a writer? The electronic monster spews out its own version of the story's ending.

"DEATH —THE INEVITABLE INTRUDER— LURKS EVERYWHERE, IN PUBLIC BUILDINGS, EVEN IN THE PLACID DREAMS OF INNOCENT CHILDREN. THIS AGE OF TECHNOLOGY, EXPLODING ATOMS, AIR POLLUTION, SPACE EXPLORATION, CEMENT AND PLASTICS HAS OPENED THE INSATIABLE APPETITE OF CRIME, WHEREBY PROGRESS VOMITS DROVES OF VICIOUS AND PITILESS CRIMINALS. COMES TO MIND THE NIGHTMARE OF ATLANTA BETWEEN 1979 AND 1980 WITH THIRTY-NINE CHILDREN DEAD; THE MASSACRE OF SOME 360 VICTIMS OF A CERTAIN LUCAS WHOSE SMILING FACE IS SHOWN ON TELEVISION every time he shows authorities where he buried his victims' remains; over twenty decomposed bodies exhumed in the beaches of Galveston, Texas; Manson and his repulsive murders; the attack against Eden Pastora, commander Zero, on the border of Costa Rica and Nicaragua, with a final count of eight dead and innumerable more wounded. All of which proves without a doubt that crime is rampant and spares no one. When we turn on the radio or TV set, the first news we hear are the day's fatalities. The same is true of newspapers and magazines. Today it's a child raped by a pedophile or satyr. Tomorrow an innocent, quiet couple or a helpless old man. By month's end, a whole family is slaughtered with the exception of a baby that sleeps quietly in a remote place in the house, ignorant of the horror of the massacre.

Due to so much violence, upon returning home the day before, the writer checked as carefully as usual that the door to the garden was well secured with double locks in place. Because her husband was on business in Europe, she had to stay alone several days. The next evening, while she worked on her computer, the writer felt a presence in the yard that soon appeared clearly in her studio's window. A heavy set, dark man with a sadistic smile on his insolent thick lips, held in his bear-like, hairy hand a set of her own keys, the keys to her own house ringing metallically as he shook them. The writer recognized them immediately because the plastic keyholder displayed her initials in one-inch-tall silver letters. In the beginning, she didn't understand. Paralyzed by terror, she couldn't grasp the situation. Deeply distressed, eyes bulging, she first looked at the sheet of paper she had just gotten from the computer, and then turned toward the window. She finally understood what happened with the keys: when she returned the day before, tired and worried by the crazy behavior of her youngest daughter, she inadvertently left the key outside in the lock...and later, believing that she was protecting herself from an intruder, she locked the double locks from the inside! In the meantime, the keys on the outside lock became an irresistible temptation to the intruder. At that moment, a click released the first lock while the radio announced that an image of the Virgin, recently brought from Italy, was shedding real tears —someone had tasted them and they were salty— She asked herself anxiously if what was happen-

ING MIGHT BE PART OF THE STORY SHE HAD STARTED PRINTING FROM THE MEMORY OF THE COMPUTER, EARLY THAT MORNING..."

She knew the rest because her final destiny was forever recorded in the bottomless abyss of the electronic monster, the identity usurper. She could only curl up in the corner of the studio. Then, with infinite sadness she looked at the back of her numerous books, the unanswered letters, the beautiful original paintings that filled her retinas with color... everything appeared so lonely and sad while she waited for the intruder. She heard the slight ringing of the keys as the man tried the second lock. After an endless pause, she heard the second click.

According to the ending that the electronic monster devised for the story — one that Rita Creso never finished — she knew that it would be useless to run into hiding, scream, call the neighbors for help, call the police. Everything would be in vain. Any effort would be worthless. Crouching on the floor, listening intently to the passages of Mozart's REQUIEM, broadcast by Radio KLEF, the monumental concert that the Austrian composer could not finish because Salieri defeated him—that monster of murderous jealousy—Rita Creso, still petrified, waited for the intruder to open the door and step in.

The Peace Brigade

Can lovers meet and exchange kisses on battle-fields still acrid with bomb fumes?

Will the poet compose his songs under stars veiled in gun smoke?

Will the musician strum his lute in a night whose silence was ravished by terror?

Kahil Gibran

They waited. Entrenched, feeling the anxiety that precedes an imminent battle like a fist of fear stuck in the throat they waited for the enemy, their rifles ready to repel the attack. Since early morning they had lost contact with command headquarters. Nevertheless, their instinct told them that the still invisible enemy was huge in numbers and had been patrolling the fields around them. At day break, distant rumblings shook the earth under their feet. The rumblings seemed to belong to a hundred thousand feet advancing toward them with death clung to their boots, with death in their uniforms, setting their weapons for accurate marksmanship against them, their enemies. Besides, all through the morning, while still stay in touch with command headquarters, they had been instructed to keep watch while waiting for a multitude of adversaries advancing toward their camp.

Anxiety made them thirsty. With terror they found that their ears had become so oversensitive that they could detect the slightest sound among the confusing tempo of their collective beating hearts, which sounded gloomily in their chests and echoed thunderously in their craniums. They could assess the intensity of their terror by the constant depth of their slow, rhythmic breathing, like an animal in ambush... ready to strike... perhaps... They perceived it in the tumultuous hubbub of disjointed dialogues, the... Shit! Now we're caught in a trap, in the middle of this flat field, without a single way to take cover!

"Well, we might as well place our souls in the hands of God, because nobody'll come out alive from this battle... even if he fights like the bravest of machos..."

"Damn it! I'd been dreaming of taking leave this week to see my wife and kids!'

"And I already had authorization to quit forever. What rotten luck!"

"Will any of us survive from this battle? No doubt the enemy is far stronger in numbers and we... we're no more than a fistful of men with scarcely any ammunition."

"You're right, man! Holy shit!, this is getting ugly. None of us will survive."

Among all these melded sounds, in the most distant horizon, semi-diluted in the light of a sunset tinted red like a harbinger of tragedy, they started to perceive the mumbling of singing voices growing closer. Who could sing in the midst of such terror that stretched nerves as taut as violin strings? They looked at each other perplexed, unable to understand, still searching for an explanation; it's a bad sign, they said, because if the enemy sings it means that he is sure of victory.

"It's an ambush. Yea, an ambush."

"A gigantic wave of enemies."

"While we're just a tiny handful of scarcely fifty men, poorly equipped and with hardly any ammunition."

"What a bitch! We'll die for sure, no doubt about it."

"This isn't an army of enemies, partners, it's death itself trotting toward us!"

"The horsemen of the Apocalypse."

On the horizon, the rustle of marching steps grew increasingly louder in the twilight of the setting sun. Among the shadows that absorbed trees, rocks, the Eastern mountains, the creek, everything, the enemies' voices echoed, raised in a triumphant hymn, resounded all over the sierra.

Fear grabbed at their throats like a claw of thirst. Their hearts filled with terror, burst out of their breasts to pound on their temples like a drumming funeral.

As the sun sank behind the mountains, they saw, very far way, a huge, immense, gigantic mass slowly advancing, always singing, singing, singing... but the song, still distant, still wasn't anything but a knot of mumbling.

"What are they singing?"

"Who knows..."

"The enemy must be sure of victory to be singing, because the tone is festive with no traces of a military march."

"Fifty poor devils massacred by that human mass. Thousands and thousands of them. Are you aware of it?"

Following the captain's orders they loaded their rifles and set their sights. The attack preparations were paused when they saw the white flags waved by the enemy.

"You bastards! Don't you see that it's a trick devised to save time?" The captain shrieked angrily. "Just take a look at the thousands and thousands in their ranks, and consider the small size of our platoon. If we yield to them, those white flags will be our shrouds. Attention! Aim...!"

The hymn that advanced from the red sunset heavy with presages of tragedy, made them watchful again while the ocean of shadows came nearer amidst the rustling of a devastating wave.

"Aim! Fire!" came the order in the dark and the response was a resounding blast while the echo seemed to carry far away the word "death... death... death..." A multitude of bodies fell lifeless, but those that had been spared continued to march like a gigantic mass inflamed by the strange chanting.

Excited by the firings and the victory that they already considered theirs, the warriors paid no attention to the song and let themselves be deafened by the gun's clamor. Only when the last enemies retreated in disarray, leaving a few wounded behind who still sang, the soldiers recognized the lyrics.

"They ask for peace! Peace! They sing for peace!" they all exclaimed.

When in the shadows of night they turned their flashlights toward the mounds of corpses, a shiver of horror overwhelmed all of them.

"Women! Only women! Helpless women with no weapons but a song of love and peace!" they burst out in a scream that tore into the fertile womb of mother earth.

While they cried for shame of the despicable crime committed out of fear and submission to the captain's orders, communication with command headquarters was reestablished and amidst their own wailing and curses they heard a voice announcing the "wonderful news about a peace brigade of volunteers —mothers, sisters, wives, brides, students, workers— who roam the battlefield singing the hymn of "Peace and Love to the World!" They walk into the battlefields winning the hearts of friends and enemies. Brave women, turned into ambassadors of peace, the last hope to avoid the extinction of the human race on the planet... For this reason the high command encourages everyone, friends and foes, to lay down their weapons and join these courageous women. 'Peace and love in the world!' Hail to the peace brigade! Viva!"

Hell

To Eva, my beloved daughter.

The devil is he who denies the world any rational meaning. As is well known, the world' s dominion is shared by angels and demons. Nevertheless, the world' s welfare does not require that angels defeat devils (as I believed in my childhood) but rather both their powers must be more or less balanced If there is in the world too much undisputable sense (the angels dominion) man perishes under its weight. If the world makes no more sense (the demons' control) one can neither survive in it.

Milan Kundera

She was tired of routine. She was exhausted from repeating the same actions daily from morning till night. She was weary that, from the depth of times as remote as her childhood, her person was implacably multiplied in every reflection. She was fed up with the monotony aggravated by the needless tensions of daily life.

Unable to tolerate such boredom, in one powerful stroke of her whole being, she broke the smoothness of her routine which exploded in an irrepressible chaos of shattered crystals.

From then on, her whole being was heaven: her voice was full of butterflies, birds, stars, fish, children, clowns, laughter. Her step unsure, due to so many years on the way to old age, had now gained purpose on the path of freedom asshe followed the trails of musical scales to reach the perfection of dance.

Set in the perimeters of silence for many years, her hearing burst into a kingdom of warbling, violins, sobs, clamors, cries, choruses, symphonies.

To her face, crisscrossed by a net of wrinkles and fissures, the magic of reflections lent it the purity, smoothness and joy of adolescents.

Then, unconcerned, she gave her first love and kisses to a handsome sailor who buried both in the sea. Then, she gave her love and kisses to many, and still to many more, who in turn reciprocated with deception and pain, deception and pain.

Later, after many years, she frequented bars leaving on the arm of a man, then another and many more. Still later she waited for them in sordid streets. That's how a mountain of men went through her bed and the love she dreamed about in her empty spinster's old age turned into a handful of prostituted money that could never compensate and fill up the abyss of her loneliness.

One day, in a fit of nausea, she closed her eyes tightly wishing with all her might to regress through the path of her freedom to the monotonous routine of old age that she had shunned that morning. She wanted to rebuild the routine by putting together the broken crystals she had herself shattered a few hours ago.

She wanted to stay tame and passive in the reality of her old age that hastened toward death's loneliness and absence of love.

Her effort was in vain; the dream that had penetrated the paths of freedom closed its gates and left her forever stranded in the remote past which was briefly heaven but turned swiftly into hell...

An Ephemeral Star

Despair weakens our sight and closes our ears. In despair we can see nothing but spectres of doom and can hear only to the beating of our agitating hearts.

Kahil Gibran

That early morning, like every other dawn which had been so hard to bear in her lonely old age as it had been for the last years — her bones hurt to the marrow; in sleepless nights a murderous claw clutched her heart; and the disconsolate pain of continuing to live was the unavoidable reality that stabbed at her existence— she looked out of the kitchen window while swallowing a potion for her arthritis which left no bone untouched in her frail skeleton. Suddenly she experienced a strange relief, as though emotions and hopes of her youth, put aside an eternity ago, had come again to life stimulating her decrepit existence.

"A star! A morning star," she thought with the wonder of a child who reacts happily even to the first signs of spring. So long ago —she didn't even remember when— she had searched the sky for the magic of yesterday's stars and the brightness of the Milky Way which shone in the transparency of nights above her distant village! Now the huge city's polluted air and the arrogant height of the skyscrapers wouldn't let her see but a tiny piece of sky from her window. From this opening toward the North, it was almost impossible to get a glimpse of the cottony texture of a cloud breaking the grey monotony of the atmosphere soiled every day by factories' tall chimneys and the oil refineries' emissions.

So when she saw the star, she became delighted in the resurgence of an emotion she thought had been dead in her soul, she controlled her quickened breathing to avoid unbalancing her heart rate, "because you know, Mrs. Amparo, any emotion may strain your weak heart. No excitements, neither strong nor slight! You must live quietly, in silence, without getting into arguments. You will see then how much you can prolong your life," had warned her doctor a thousand and one times. But can you call it life if it's spent in sheer dullness, with neither pleasures nor emotions? Why prolong it? What's the point of living as though dead and without any purpose? How wonderful to get excited, emotional, fill one's eyes and soul with the sight of that star in the horizon! The first one after many years... it will help me go on living till the end ever so near, without the discouragement that makes me drag my feet and slouch. Absurd, utterly absurd! Only those who already lack everything, who have nothing left in life to fall back on, can clutch on to something so small...as the emotion of seeing a star... as though this were the first star of Genesis... those who are not aware that I need this star to avoid sinking in the bottomless pit of my last days on earth might laugh at this. The star... a bird warbling... the wind whispering through the bushes... everything that lives and breathes, that shines and gives light, all of it I need to feed my hope to reach the end without the despair of living a lifeless life. What if I only dreamed the Northern star to save myself? A semblance of a star to fool the reality in which I can't find a trace of a salvation? Semblance, fantasy, appearance of a star... dream... who cares? Today I need the star to remain linked to something until I die... death that is taking so long to come.

When she hadn't the slightest doubt that, yes, the star was there offering the beckoning net of its light so her hope may reach out to life, the brightness of the star suddenly intensified. It became so large, so enormous, that, like in a nightmare, it broke boundaries and rushed with lightning speed toward her window. Truly, that couldn't be reality! Dream... Illusion... Nightmare... What else could it be? Yet it was absolute reality; but it turned out that her star of hope never was a star. The strong lights of a landing plane getting ready to descend in a military base where no air traffic had been evident for years, provided her with enough of her own reality, now fed only by her imagination, fantasies and mirages for the sole purpose and hope to continue living... living alive... living on, even by the ephemeral stirrings of an equally ephemeral emotion... till death came to her.

The Libel of Dismissal

When a man hath taken a wife and marries her, and it came to pass that she find no favour in his eyes [...] then let him write her a bill of divorcement and give it in her hand and send her out of his house...

Deuteronomy 24:1-4
King James Version

She made half a turn in bed. A movement that was her signal to him that the discussion was over and she wanted to sleep.

Of course it also meant, "Don't even dream about it, you son of a bitch, that after so many years of sacrifices and working like a slave, I should give you a divorce. You're barking up the wrong tree. And much less now, so that a shitty whore can take advantage of all I've sweated. Just remember that you haven't put in a whit of effort to get what we have. I, only I, have slaved in the beauty parlor to put bread on the table, dress Marquitos, pay for his school and also help pay your tuition so that you could graduate as a pharmacist. And now that you have your pharmacy and we can live comfortably, buy that small house that I've dreamed to have for Marquitos, — now, you bastard — now that you don't need me — this stupid moron, anymore, you tell me, 'I'm sorry, Ana, my dearest Anitica, but I can't continue living with you because, I must confess, I've fallen in love with another woman and I can't be unfaithful to you. A divorce, only a divorce will solve the problem'."

This was a recurring scene that, with some variations, always started when it was time to retire. Always when she was exhausted after having to put up with the silly whims of Mrs. Vargas who wanted her bun so and her curls thus; the stupidity of the Rodriguez woman constantly dissatisfied with her hairdo; and the exasperating shallow chatter of Lucilla, the other hairdresser. The argument always started when her nervous system was most sensitive and she had to rely on sleeping pills to avoid insomnia.

This time —breaking the habit of starting an endless discussion— when she reached the peak of her irritation, he just said to her, "It's all right. It's all right, Ana, so you don't want a divorce, there will be no divorce. Happy now? It's better that we don't destroy each other like wild animals. Let's continue the stupid farce of our marriage."

When she turned her back on him, her consciousness vaguely recorded a subreptitious smile on his face upon saying this. At first she paid scant attention to her husband's furtive smirk, but later, little by little the image of his almost jubilant acceptance gradually set in.

Of course he must be scheming some fiendish plot, otherwise why would he yield so pleasingly? What will he do next..? I have no doubt that he is planning something... Kill me? Bah! One only sees that in movies and mystery novels. Before, I had harmony and almost happiness in my marriage. We were always kidding! I remember how we laughed when I read to him the lover's column in Vanidades.

"A HUSBAND PROMOTES HIS WIFE'S QUALIFICATIONS AS A VALUABLE PRODUCT!"

How did he put it? Ah! We laughed until tears ran down our cheeks. "HUSBAND WILLING TO GIVE UP THIRTYISH WIFE" *was the headline.* "I AM WILLING TO GIVE UP MY THIRTYISH (ALMOST FORTYISH) WIFE TO ANY MAN SHE CHOOSES BECAUSE I ONLY WANT HER HAPPINESS. AFTER THE HUMILIATION AND FRUSTRATION OF BEING EXILED FROM OUR NUPTIAL BED, I WOULD LIKE TO FEEL FREE ONCE MORE TO LOVE SOMEONE, TO ENJOY A NEW AND PERHAPS LAST PASSION. WOULD YOU PLEASE SUGGEST TO ME A WAY TO DISCREETLY DIVULGE THAT MY WIFE IS AVAILABLE? IF MY ANNOUNCEMENT WERE TO BE SUCCESSFUL, THE AUTUMNAL YEARS OF THREE CITIZENS SHALL BE ENRICHED. *It was signed* 'I MEAN IT'." *When the news surfaced about the criminal who laced Tylenol with strychnine and poisoned a number of people, everything was fine between us, and we used to laugh together and kid each other affectionately. I sometimes said to him teasingly that it would be easy for him to eliminate me without anybody suspecting him.*

> *"Look, Timothy, in this medicine cabinet where I keep my sleeping capsules, I also have capsules to kill rats... they're the same shape and size. You'd only have to switch the bottles and... bang!, your wife's gone, because when I can't sleep at night I reach desperately for what I need to overcome insomnia and no one can ever make me turn on the light. I go to the cabinet touching the furniture to find my way and since I know by heart what's in every shelf (here to the right, the sleeping pills, next to them the moisturizer, behind it, the rat poison). I instantly swallow the capsules in the dark." At the time, as gently as he had premiered my virginity, Tim used to answer.*
>
> *"You are making a mistake, Anita, you are wrong. You should put the rat poison in a different place to avoid a fatal mishap."*
>
> *For fear of Marquitos touching the rat poison, by inertia, who knows! I left it in the cabinet... They say that we all seek and create our own des...ti...ny. But the poison is in a safer place in the cabinet, high up, out of Marquitos' reach.*

We haven't joked around for a long time. Our bedroom atmosphere is thick with insidious arguments and everything revolves around divorce, divorce and more divorce. The sleeping capsules... two, I took two cap-su-les... di-vor-ce... Divorce and death! What if he switched the bottles, and I, stupid, moronic me... possessed by rage after the discussion, feeling my way in the dark, swallowed the rat poison? It's still time. I can get up... take an antidote, look for the note I wrote to him the first time he asked for a divorce. "Tim, my dear, after what happened today I have nothing left in the world and I only want to die. What would be the purpose of continuing to live when nothing makes sense to me anymore?" My own words would justify his crime and the bastard could get away smelling like a rose. "I only desire death," I wrote to him because that's how I felt. But to kill myself... I would have to be crazy! What I meant was a Christian kind of death by natural causes, following God's designs. I'm tired, sickened, fed up, yes, FED UP from fighting so hard... what for? Just to end up, sooner or later, like everyone else rotting in a hole.

* * *

She then makes an effort to get up. The antidote and the message are her only obsessions. The capsule is already working and a heavy sleepiness holds her down on the mattress. She tries to move her hands, but they don't obey her will... as though they belonged to another body. She tries hard to open her eyes and for the last time look at the room that was a witness to so many happy times with him, but the heaviness that pervades her body keeps them shut. She tries to scream but she can't open her lips sealed by lethargy. She is under total, heavy drowsiness. The ultimate outcome is imminent and definitive. The outcome? Did she really swallow rat poison? She had always longed for a placid, serene death, at dusk, when the sun displays its triumphant spectrum of lights in an infinite horizon... the death of someone who had lived fully. Now she can barely control her anxiety and accept death once and for all. Is she really going to die? How similar are death and sleep! In the conviction that there is nothing else she can do, she lets herself go in a beautiful skiff decorated with garlands redolent of roses and jasmines. She lets herself go down river, down river, down river... slowly, very slowly... amid images at times frozen in space. Suddenly, mixed with the river's whispering, she hears Timothy's robust, overpowering snoring, at her side, very close to her. She tries in vain to move a hand, waken him from deep sleep and ask for help. Not a particle of her body obeys her efforts... and right there, within reach of her hand, Timothy snores peacefully, unaware that she slips down river in the beautiful skiff overflowing with roses and jasmines, down river... down river... toward the abyss opening its monstrous black, frightening mouth... while her husband's indifferent snoring resounds as a murderous spear of thunder, undisturbed in deepest, relaxed slumber.

She lets herself be dragged to the abyss while holding back a scream stuck like a knot in her throat. Sinking in disturbing blackness, she asks herself how the murderer can sleep so blissfully and snore at her side. Could she be dreaming? What if it were all nothing but a nightmare and tomorrow...? Tomorrow? What if to-mo-rrow... she wa-kes...u...u...up?

Pythagoras' Illustrious Disciple

To Lauderlina Longhi, my unforgettable teacher.

Reality likes symmetries and slight anachronisms.

Jorge Luis Borges

The truth is that when he entered the office he didn't expect the surprises that awaited him. The little man, manager of the store, invited him to sit down in the most uncomfortable armchair upholstered in cheap red vinyl that crackled at his slightest movements — even the often unnoticed rhythm of his breathing made it creak... rather squeak. It suddenly occurred to him that such a sensitive piece of furniture was there so his owner might detect his clients' reactions from a distance. He smiled. No doubt about it, television programs full of suspense, electronic spying gadgets, tapped telephones and other forms of human behavior control permeated his daily life and almost inevitably played paranoic tricks on him. Before leaving home, the challenging pages of Orwell's Animal Farm had scared and worried him, just as shortly before the desolate vision of the future as portrayed in Ayn Rand's novel *Anthem...*

> *Yes, it's true that we live in a democratic country, why doubt it? Nonsense! Many ways abound of shackling our freedom and periodically limiting the areas of our ephemeral activities abound! Before we realize it we have become paranoiacs... and myself, like most other bastards, am almost about to join the ranks. It's best to laugh at my paranoid manias... start reading other crap, watch different TV programs...! Is it really possible to establish a selective policy in our violence ridden society, with the powers that be and so much bullshit? To hell with speculations! The world will not be magically straightened out because I stick my fingers in its wounds! Besides, my word is not endowed with the healing powers of a shaman.*

The little man had left my friend waiting in his office while he tried to find the suit he had ordered to his measurements. So as to avoid any further digressions, he focussed on scrutinizing the office space where he had been relegated for quite a while. Wide windows framed the striking deep blue of La Carpintera mountains, that from their majestic heights transmitted an irresistible desire to leaping off to their tallest peaks and fly to the heavens. He realized that the wait — any waiting in his life — derailed his thoughts from to the extreme to the plainly absurd. The best thing for him to do was to anchor his attention on his surroundings (he had turned this into a standard procedure to avoid getting carried away by his wild imagination). Unfortunately, in the present situation, much to his mortification, the most atrocious, dubious or deplorable taste prevailed; a taste that utterly strangled the generous space of the open window against the splendor of his beloved mountains to the infinite blue beyond. On top of the canary-yellow desk, plastic flowers splattered with fly droppings were displayed in a vase bought, for sure, in the dinkiest, dirtiest stand of the Central Market. The rest of the furniture, upholstered in the same squeaking material that revealed its hostile disposition, made him shrink inside, as though his inner-self had the power to protect him from such aesthetic crime. No pictures hung from the walls, not even the interesting posters so fashionable everywhere, but the cheapest, most faded lithographs, also covered by the diarrheic splattering of flies; among them, in a violently baroque frame, stood out a brand new and striking certificate issued by the National Chamber of Commerce acknowledging the highest quality of services and merchandise of the "Almacenes Universales, S.A." Everything was so appallingly vulgar that no one could even suspect that the withered man, (dried-up and diminutive, he gave the painful impression of being smothered by the presence of the store's merchandise— shirts, socks, ties, shorts, suits and jackets) who had kept him waiting for so long, could have such a surprise for him. Well, it's best not to reveal the punch line, rather start the story from the beginning, in the proper sequence, event after event, just the way my friend told it to me.

From the tailor's department of "Almacenes Universales, S.A." he had mistakenly received a suit that neither in color nor size matched the one he had ordered for a reception at the Department of Culture. So he went to see the manager of the store hoping to retrieve the right suit that he would wear to the party. The manager —dried-up, minuscule, hollow-chested— talked to him with the calculated courtesy that puts distance between people, as is customary among high-ranking employees who want to stay on friendly terms with clients. He looked at him with the common gaze of merchants and businessmen who never leave their hovels and only think of the figure they will charge on an invoice for a substantial profit or to increase their bank accounts. When he stretched his hand (soft, moist, clammy and repulsive) something in that pygmy made him surreptitiously hide under his arm the edition of Homer he had just acquired because he had the strange feeling that neither his book nor himself had the right to be in that place. He, with his artistic-literary manias, and the book were an insult to the spiritual, aesthetic and physical flatness of that homunculus and dismal hole which he inhabited systematically every day for more than eight hours, except Sundays (how my friend despised the hell out of routine!). He subconsciously attempted to wipe out the sensation of vertigo transmitted by the touch of the limp, moist, repulsive hand with his handkerchief. He was instantly aware of the futility of his gesture, because the feeling of dizziness increased later, when upon taking leave, the little man pronounced his name adding the usual "at your service..." According to my friend, office, papers, invoices, desks, files and everything else that reeks of pen pushers and management, sadly transforms all those who deal with them into neutered and ill-defined beings. To him their nullifying effect changes their voices... that guy actually spoke in a toneless and effeminate manner. His metamorphosis also manifested itself in his way of dressing without any personal identity that may have raised him to the category of a unique and irreplaceable human being... at a level with only a few select personalities.

When the little man stretched out his hand (soft, moist and repulsive as a leach), to say good-bye, he repeated his name adding the customary "at your service for anything you wish," the feeling of vertigo really overwhelmed my friend. It was then that, still incredulous, he asked the guy to repeat his name.

"Paris. Paris of Troy, at your service."

"Ah! Eh! You... Paris of Troy?" My friend looked at him astounded, unable to dispel his amazement. The truth is that everything would have continued normally and without any consequences if that afternoon, among silly, inconsequential news (as reported daily) he had not read about Martin Barret, an American athlete who was taking his place among the most outstanding football stars. The extraordinary thing about this was that his name and detailed biography, including trophies, studies, titles, were mentioned in an obscure encyclopedia on sports dating almost a hundred years ago... even his daguerreotype showed a young man with the same facial structure as Barret... and they were not even relatives. That morning my friend and I had talked about such a fascinating case.

Who knows why, today I'm just thinking bullshit! In this world of wrenching realities, about daily bread to place on the family's table, of people starving to death, jobless workers walking the streets, a war in Iraq an American or Russian intervention in Central America, forty thousand dead in demonstrations in El Salvador, the persistent talk of the possible use of nuclear weapons while the horror of Hiroshima's anniversary is celebrated (yes, celebrated! How morbid!). We are unable to shake off all these horrors just by turning our backs, yet I busy myself with all this shit about a fool that today, after a century —or who knows how long ago— shows up with identical traits and background of someone who died, positively passed way, innumerable years ago. Just as a chain stretched out indefinitely... in-de-fi-ni-tely. Bastard! Come to think of it... Who am I cloned after?

To snap out of his amazement, in an attempt at humor, he quoted the words printed in the just bought Homer, the book he held under his arm.

"Paris of Troy... the one Herodote calls Alexander, God knows why! The one who appeared to his mother in a dream as the torch that would burn down Troy... the one who abducted Helen, the beautiful, seductive married woman... the one who fled with her and thus divided two families in a cruel, everlasting feud... I said two..."

The weakling looked at my friend with shifty eyes; his voice and gestures were also disjointed and erratic as he interrupted.

"Sir, control yourself. Do I meddle in your private life which would give you the right to meddle in mine?" His defensive aggressiveness was obvious. "Did her husband send you after me? I mean, Helen's husband, under the pretext of claiming the damn suit you bought in our store? Confess!"

These last words were pronounced with great emphasis, almost in a scream. All the while sweat was running in streams down his face. He wouldn't stop shrieking like a troll.

"Helen's husband persecutes me, he has harassed me an eternity and he tells everybody in the world that he won't leave me alone until he sees Helen's bones, mine and my family's in the grave... I flee because of her, to protect her and avoid a senseless massacre... yes, I have been fleeing for an eternity.. Understand this and take pity on me... on us all! As to the story about me torching our hacienda, Troy, it happened in my youth... it was almost a childish mischief, a prank if you wish... it ruined my family and this is the reason why I have to earn my living as a clerk, instead of being a grandee, as befits the noble rank of my name.

In our country, claims of nobility ring as wild fantasies, thought my friend. Nevertheless, he made no objection because at that precise moment he had the impression that the despicable subordinate attributes of the little man had disappeared and instead he suddenly seemed imbued of manly strength, beauty and forcefulness, almost, almost as a real homeric Paris should be; his body seemed to emit a mysterious brightness as though his skin were impregnated in oceanic sun rays. And to think that he had judged him all the time as a foolish jackanape, soft and pale as an oyster!

At that moment, when the little man's voice was pitched high with imminent premonitions of death, he, having his hand on the door's handle and ready to leave in a hurry, froze. He sank in timeless time while the figure of Paris appeared clearly under the Tree of Discord —Accursed trees that repeat endlessly stories of sin and evil!— It was offering the golden apple—another reprehensible chain reaction since Genesis— to beautiful Venus, thus sparking condemnations from rejected Hera and Pallas Athena.

"Why does a respectable gentleman like you tolerate the vileness of a man such as Menelao, jealous as an Othello stripped of dignity?"

"Haven't you more serious business to undertake in your position in government...? Are you just another political appointee like so many idle fools in government positions? Haven't you a family and children to look after so you may leave me alone with my Helen?"

My friend tried to reply that he had said what he did just for the heck of it, because it was written like that in the book he carried under his arm, and his intellectual urge to boast about his knowledge had made him utter such tripe (which he, personally, considered fabulous myths). However, instead of giving this explanation he recalled the images of enrage, wildly mad Hera and Athena at Tetis and Peleo's wedding. He couldn't help himself.

"Forgive me. Please, forgive me. I didn't know that the legendary curse set at the famous beauty contest would be inexorably *repeated ad infinitum.*"

"What damned curse are you talking about?" His voice had a thundering force which again gave him the appearance of a mythical hero.

"So you also know, you infamous busybody, that in a beauty contest in which I was a member of the jury, I rejected two daughters of prominent families in the city so that I could give my vote to the loveliest Adita, the one with the complexion as sweet and fair as dawn's light. That's why... But why should I explain anything to you, damned meddler from hell! I'm sure that you already know how those Harpies piled up curses on me. What an idiot I am! Worse than an idiot! He started to pound the canary yellow desk, throw papers up in the air and hurl objects to the floor.

He was possessed by the demons of rage and he kept repeating with sparks of hate in his eyes, "Helen... Helen... Helen..." Helen here, there and yonder. He wasn't even aware that my indiscreet friend had slipped away unnoticed like a wisp of smoke.

I was walking into the store when I ran into my friend. Just by the tone of his "hello" I realized that he was deeply disturbed, as though his spirit had entered a field of alienation within which his whole being had been shaken to its deepest roots.

"Hey, man, is something the matter? Are you sick?" I asked worried. He was pale, distracted, sweating, and all of his harmoniously muscular body was inexplicably trembling.

"Nothing, it's nothing. Come on, asshole, and listen to me so you can get this through your skull for the rest of your life. Learn from my experience, which is highly valuable of course. Listen, I have once more confirmed the wisdom of the Greeks thanks to another pythagorean axiom. Son of a bitch! My mother was right when she repeated time and time again that we pay for our sins by suffering on this earth the punishments of hell. I, stubborn as I am, believed she said that in her conviction about the biblical valley of tears because she hadn't even finished high school. But that wasn't it. Now I understand that she was a graduate in the unique sect of the chosen few... and I, naturally sucked it from her breast."

"I don't know what you're talking about, idiot. Could you explain?" In amazement, I stared at him and started noticing a strangely abnormal look in his eyes. Under the excitement of his discourse he mispronounced the words that ran into each other chaotically. He never gave me a chance to say anything. He told me in one breath, without a single pause as though he were in a big rush, everything that had happened previously. Then he suddenly grabbed me by the lapels.

"Look, do you see that insignificant little man who is now leaving the parking lot, the one with the red tie? Well, that one, yes, that thing (because he hardly deserves being called a man) that is Paris of Troy... Just as Pythagoras taught us, human life is a process of atonement, the punishment for a past life... if we apply arithmetology, and if there is a harmonious coincidence of spaces in the seven tones of the musical octave and the seven planets, in the long run this degraded Paris also keeps pace with the cosmic harmony. According to the pythagorian table of opposites, it's obvious that Paris was reduced to the unlimited, the plurality, the darkness and the evil, to atone for the many mistakes he accumulated in each existence one century after another. Yes, now I see clearly why the number 6, which stands for imperfection, is on his office door.

I couldn't snap out of my amazement. The last nonsensical sentences he muttered made me sadly realize that what we had started as a foolish obsession of pythagorianism was manifest in him like a worrisome neurosis. He repeated all that nonsense in our conversations, but in a mood of philosophical banter, without the anxiety expressed in his voice... without the metaphysical nausea that now surfaced in his eyes. Trying not to exacerbate him, I listened patiently, rather, I made him believe that I listened.

"Today I've had a revelation that will be my salvation and can also save all those who follow the infinite designs in which I'm merely a slightest of dots. I have just found justification for my life. My efforts shall amend the erroneous outline in the schema that is part of my life. I renounce the hedonistic dissoluteness of wild sprees, cheap women, liquor, vices and selfishness. From now on, I shall lead an exemplary life to amend the whole outline of my existence. When reincarnation occurs in the future, it should follow the line in the series that reaches for perfection. A hard task, I know, because it depends on many circumstances, but we shall see. Now, take heed of my encounter today, face to face, with one of those creatures that atones dearly and miserably for his many past lives during which he repeated mistakes and continues to multiply transgressions until someone like myself, the Messiah, changes the schema. I must go right away to plan the perfect transformation of the model, since I have been selected by destiny. Not everybody can see himself as I do, in the mirror image of another.

"But..." I dared to object. "You forget that the theory of metempsychosis implies the atonement of sins in other bodies striving for perfection... and degradations of such magnitude aren't even mention...?"

He didn't let me finish. He just took the time to tap me affectionately on the shoulder. Nevertheless, he paused a second and gave me his usual mischeivious look when I yelled at him in my habitual jestful greeting.

"Bye! See you tomorrow, Hipodamus of Mileto, illustrious disciple of Pythagoras!"

That evening, while I was drinking at the Swiss Chalet bar, I was horrified to hear the news of my friend's fatal accident... It happened just fifteen minutes after leaving the entrance to Almacenes Universales! His Lincoln Continental crashed into a truck driving against traffic and was turned into scrap iron.

Shocked, I felt as if my body emptied itself and turned into soft matter spread on the tall bar stool. I faced the kind of death one can never accept, when only minutes before we were together and said "Bye! See you tomorrow." Poor guy! He never had a chance to perfect a schema and much less reach the perfection of odd numbers... So he'll continue to atone for an eternity... Will I have the time and opportunity to improve the schema to which I belong?

Intergalactic Crusade

When he had opened the sixth seal, I looked, there was a great earthquake: and the sun became black as sackcloth of hair, and the full moon became as blood: and the stars of heaven fell unto the earth even as a fig tree casteth her untimely figs when she is shaken of mighty wind. And the heaven departed as a scroll when it is rolled up together: and every mountain and island were removed out of their places. And the kings of the earth, and the great men and the rich men, and the chief captains, and every freeman, hid themselves in the dens and in the rocks of the mountains; and said to the mountains and rocks; "Fall on us, and hide us from the face of him that sitteth on the throne, and from the wrath of the Lamb: for the great day of his wrath is come, and who shall be able to stand?

Revelation, 6:12-17
King James' Version

Considering the meticulous inspection of planets, stars and satellites that I describe in detail so that your Supreme Spaciality gets an idea of the domains encompassed by the Galactic Empire and the infinite wealth it owns; and considering the following reasons, it is necessary to end this official report with a recommendation to waste no more time or extremely valuable resources from the spacial power in aiding the last planet on the list assigned to the team under my command.

The first time we contacted its inhabitants, it was a wealthy planet, prosperous, creative, fully blossoming. Its surrounding atmosphere was a complex map of airways constantly streaked by planes in all sizes which flew over the irregular surface landscaped by prairies, craters and mountains. A real promise to the expansionist policy of the Galactic Empire. Nevertheless, its inhabitants, those miserably horrendous creatures (according to our standards, rather deformed) dominated by the most vile passions inconceivable under the system of perfection that prevails among us, have led it to disaster.

Attesting to the depressing physical inferiority of these creatures, I must stress that they shiver and freeze to death in temperatures even we could stand without a coat; and, even if the most insignificant fiery star comes close to their sphere, they choke until they die of the heat. We must acknowledge that they gave tangible proof of extraordinary progress in the fields of technology, architecture, sciences, art, and so on. So much so, that in some instances at the height of their development they managed to penetrate some of the secrets of our supreme wisdom, such as the atom and its powers, the laser beams, the ships that break the stratosphere barriers and visiting other planets and satellites just as our space ships do, electronic memories that they called computers, and powerful nuclear reactors. The list was long, almost endless, to the point that it even included the theory of relativity. But compared to the extent of our own knowledge, their accomplishments scarcely amount to a miserable handful of sand.

Not withstanding the limitations of these miserable creatures, their minds demonstrate a capacity to accomplish the same as those in the lowest socio-intellectual strata of our cellular organization. Obviously, they would never reach the ninth level in the social structure of our Galactic Empire, much less that of the governing selectocracy.

Spiritually, its preeminence manifests itself in clairvoyant leaders such as Solomon, Moses, Mahoma, Saul, Buddha and others. And prominent among them, Jesus the Redeemer, who changed the course of history by preaching peace and love. Nevertheless, in this despicable planet there was no room for such a perfect being and they crucified him. Later the followers of Jesus the Redeemer called themselves Christians and grew in number until they reached an overwhelming majority. Yet, only a few among them practiced his teachings of peace and love. Rather they adopted the opposite: war and hate. Thus, they crucified the Redeemer of tame preaching once more.

In order that our Supreme Spaciality may better understand the recommendation included in this report, I wish to stress the fact that instead of evolving, this planet has experienced a lamentable regression. Since I visited in 1980, approximately fifty years ago, until our present time, it has turned into a desolate and barren dessert whose surface has been ravaged by new inventions and scientific discoveries. Those miserable creatures turned the atom —the visceral element of our own daily life— into what they call the atom bomb. They did the same with the laser beam. They started a war confronting two gigantic adversaries that labeled themselves superpowers. They lied, insulted and accused each other; they persecuted and put innumerable persons in jail. They tortured and enacted terrorism, killing each other without restraint until the inevitable came to happen: the two superpowers annihilated each other, eliminating themselves from the face of the earth with their own murderous weapons.

Before that happened, the airships that once flew in the atmosphere ceased to fly because of terrorism. Since terrorism is unknown in our civilization, and I have mentioned it twice, I feel duty bound to explain its nature. It entails acts of violence and crime performed by one superpower against the other; most frequently the victims are the utterly innocent: women, children, the elderly, tranquil, harmless people who cry for peace. It thus happened that among those despicable creatures a series of revenges and terrorist actions of unimaginable magnitude occurred. For fear of kidnapppings and assassinations (at the beginning of this report and in relation to other planets, I described these revolting acts that most of our people know nothing about) the populace opted for final seclusion in their homes, which looked more like prisons because of the number of iron bars and security locks that protected them. Urban citizens ended up going out only under the protection of night's shadow to get some food so they could continue to survive.

In an act of desperation, after confirming that their way of life made no sense, the citizens of both superpowers attacked each other with the atom bomb.

The present conditions on Planet Earth are so pitiful, that I feel justified in suggesting that we send the galactic crane as a reasonable measure. It is imperative that we clean up the harmonious expanse of the Galactic Empire. This unfortunate planet not only denies our principles and striving to perfection, but also rises as a monument to stupidity and the triumph of blind passions. We must not forget that many light-years ago our Galactic Empire rejected the lowest passions to make way for sound reasoning, which prevails in the whole realm of our powers.

I have now finished the galactic inspection accomplished by myself working with the team of experts assigned to my service. This mission lasted only half a century. Having achieved this, my first mission, I trust that I fill the requirements necessary to qualify for the title of General Inspector of the Galactic Empire that is granted to the youngest in our system. I humbly hope to have satisfied our Supreme Spaciality.

Looking forward to your imperial commands, I remain your faithful servant.

Thanatos Apol'lyon

P.S. I write this postscriptum on a separate sheet of paper because I wish you would pay attention to an unofficial commentary. I am concerned about the following: among the multiple and strange beliefs of Planet Earth's native, whose destruction I recommend, I observed a curious conviction that proclaims resurrection after death of all those that follow the doctrines of Jesus the Redeemer. If this promise of resurrection becomes a reality, the imperfections so alien to our Empire would certainly be perpetuated.

On the other hand, Euphorio, the expert in spiritual evaluation on the team under my command, after thoroughly studying the teachings of Jesus the redeemer, suggests that our selectocracy adopt such doctrines in order to attain the highest levels of self-improvement.

God, love and charity are lacking in our Galactic Empire which impairs the definite excellence of our lineage, according to Euphorio.

Once More Cain and Abel

And the Lord said unto Cain, "Where is Abel thy brother?" and said "I know not: 'am I my brother's keeper?" And he said, "What hast thou done? The voice of your brother's blood crieth unto me from the ground. And now art thou cursed from the earth, which hath opened her mouth to receive thy brother's blood from thy hand.

Genesis 4:9-11
King James' Version

On both sides of the frontier the contending armies braced themselves for battle. With satisfaction, both bands' chiefs noticed that instead of the gloomy attitude of the past and the sad miens forecasting death as on previous occasions, now the soldiers projected an assertive mood, hopeful and even joyful on the eve of an imminent military action.

"These assholes are already used to the hardships of combat. Thousands, millions of battles can be won with men of such strong fighting disposition," remarked the commandant of the Sandinista faction.

Simultaneously the one on the resistance side was saying, "I have no doubt that training and discipline have erased all traces of laziness in these mother-fuckers. With such a bunch of powerful 'machos' the enemy won't have a chance to do anything, much less offer resistance."

The comments and statements about their respective assured victory, based on the healthy attitude of the soldiers, spread among the high officers of both parties. Meanwhile, the armies of the Sandinista as well as those of the resistance were getting ready for combat by digging trenches, carrying supplies, driving bullet-proof tanks and camouflaging cannons while continually singing, whistling or happily humming. Some of them even displayed a permanent smile on their faces and a light of near content in their eyes. It seemed that instead of preparing themselves for battles, they were looking forward to a feast. Once in a while they would interrupt the song on their lips, and both Sandinista and resistance soldiers would whisper in each others ears.

"Don't forget the password, asshole!"

* * *

Everything is ready for the fighting. The Sandinista and resistance high commands have taken their positions. The warriors on both sides of the frontier brace themselves for the fight, while they whisper to each other in the dead silence that pervades the atmosphere.

"The password, don't forget it. The password, man!"

The high commands are amazed that a halo of serenity seems to surround the troops, as though everyone were certain of the nearing victory. But there is always someone who expresses concern at an unusual event.

"The absence of adrenaline spewed out by fear and the lack of concern from the soldiers confronting danger could possibly blow everything to hell."

"It seems to me," another comments, "that they're high on drugs. Who knows where the hell they got the grass! It reeks of weed."

The high commands' worries gradually increase as the moment of fighting draws nearer. But they can't stop the course of events because danger is imminent.

"Atteeeention! Chaaarge! Fiiire!" The order is firmly shouted, repeated as an echo by the closest subordinates who carry it through the battlefield like a verbal wave. Upon hearing the command, the Sandinistas and contras scream with great excitement.

"The password! The password, men!" And dropping their weapons or firing in the air, they jump out of the trenches, over the machine guns and cannons and war tanks, running toward their enemies with arms outstretched. Everyone, from both sides, throws the world into a state of confusion when in a strong, fraternal embrace they simultaneously yell a sentence, endlessly repeated to satiety.

"Brothers! We are brothers! From this day on Cain and Abel are forever united..."

Confirmation of the Obvious

A man walks with the sun on his back. Long, how long the day is. Also bitter. The sun, withered orange, will settle in the West and the lemon of the moon shall give the man a glass of doubtful dreams, while the night, alas, will carry him to morning and the story will again be repeated.

Juan Cervera

In his despair the man said, "Time for action. I've reached the limit. Time has to be stopped once and for all."

He took off his wristwatch, placed it on the table and for a short while examined it as though for the first time he noticed its face and hands that continued ticking its chronometric rhythm with implacable stubbornness. A furious anxiety twisted the tense muscles of his face when he pulled out the gun. He fired... He fired making a mess of the watch.

"We must put an end to time once and for all," was his explanation.

With unabated rage, he stopped the monotonous tic-toc of the pendulum that had marked time for over a century in the hall. It marked time. It marked time, sad or happy, although ephemeral, of all and each member of the family.

"Damned time, here you are now faced by the only one who dares to stop you once and for all!" he shrieked. Then he went into every room in the house and one by one, amidst a thousand curses, he destroyed every watch and clock. Later, he went out in the street and fired at every clock he saw. After he destroyed those of the church and city hall, he became discouraged, as empty as a suit without a body, and fell apart on a bench in the square screaming.

"Who dares fight time that multiplies, multiplies forever? How can it be stopped if it doesn't cease to multiply, multiply and multiply unless we reduce the number of watches and clocks?"

Someone approached him and asked why. Why since what he just said was a truth already known and confirmed even by him, did he insist on carrying on a massacre of time? Crying without restraint, and screaming at the top of his lungs, the criminal answered.

"I'm not testing the infinity of time. Don't you see? It's my own stupidity I challenge. Only an idiot like me dares measure his vulnerable humanity against endless time! Only an asshole like me! My wife told me so today when I accused her of screwing around with every bastard in this shitty town!"

Distributive Justice

For it is easier for a camel to go through a needle's eye, than for a rich man to enter into the kingdom of God!

Luke 18:25

* * *

Again, the kingdom of heaven is like unto treasure hid in a field: the which when a man hath found, he hideth, and for joy therefore goeth and selleth all that he hath and buyeth that field.

Matthew 13:44
King James' version

Mister John Johnson, the millionaire entrepreneur who built the finest glass skyscrapers reflecting magic multicolored lights at sunset;

the one who accumulated millions and millions over unexpected turns of the market; the one who was awarded *honoris causa* doctorates by the universities he favored with his magnificent generosity; the one who, like a child swallowing a piece of candy spent on a single party what a hundred citizens would spend in a year or more; that one. That multimillionaire John Johnson suddenly found himself depressed one day. After hours of reflection, he saw himself as he had never noticed before. A sullen face, sallow complexion and dark circles under his eyes. His lips couldn't even fake a smile.

"Without any doubt," he said, "it's the millions that weigh so heavily over me. They're mercilessly crushing me." In his motivation to not die buried under the weight of onerous fortune and the mass of cement, iron, glass and metal of his buildings, he searched for every possible remedy. He consulted the pastor of his Methodist church. He visited psychologists, psychoanalists, and psychiatrists. He tried his luck with fortune-tellers who read his palms, Tarot cards and tea leaves while cleaning out his pockets. He even went to "santeros" who put him through the snail's test and danced to Xango for him but no one, absolutely no one, pointed him in the direction to solve his problem because they were too caught up in his money and cared little for the agonizing depth of the inscrutable void he faced. So he turned increasingly thin and dispirited.

At the hotel where all the world's millionaires held a sumptuous seminar on "How to multiply our investments *ad infinitum*," Mr. John Johnson could not fall asleep, his mind overflowing with figures and bond market operations. Restlessly thrashing around on his bed, as if his spiritual mange had taken over his body, he repeated to himself that all the paraphernalia and capitalist rhetoric were nonsense and a waste of time. Desperate, he turned on the light and looked for something to read. But every piece of paper in his briefcases was about interests, transactions, properties, incomes, shares and investments. On top of the night table, by the lamp, he saw the Bible and for lack of anything else he started to read with the hope of falling asleep. After reading the story of the wealthy man who asked Jesus what he must do to insure his salvation, he decided to give up everything. Skyscrapers, works of art, jewelry, glassware, gold and silver ingots, shares, bonds, bills, coins, fine rugs, in fact all the possessions that tied him to the wretched world of material treasures.

The minute he had given up all his wealth, he experienced the profoundest joy of his generosity and considered himself the luckiest human being in the world. He grew determined to place his unlimited possessions in the hands of an administrative board with the intent of funding an almost utopic hospital complex, something that had never existed before. This almost utopic hospital complex was created for the city's indigents, to give them the same care that the richest of the rich enjoyed at no cost whatsoever. Now, nobody without financial means could complain of physical ailments, lack of facilities or care because the Hospital of Perpetual Assistance was there for them like a huge monument to health, the tallest building in the city, overpowering all others like a bastion in defense of indigent patients. Besides, it was the most spacious, comfortable building of its kind, equipped with the best physicians, researchers and specialists in the entire world. Throughout its interior the most advanced technology was in use from the computers, to electronic instruments and lasser beams. Truly, the city became a model of health care and well-being. Thanks to the Hospital of Perpetual Assistance, even death seemed rather frustrated, because only on rare occasions did it show its bald cranium.

Physically reduced to a minimum and fed mostly by spiritual readings, one winter day the former multimillionaire John Johnson froze to death on a bench in Tranquility Park where he often spent the night since the lessons of the Gospel had even led him to give up his home. He was found frozen, with eyes raised fixedly to the sky and a beautiful smile that put and end to the slight surge of pity among those who found him. Some of them commented that they perceived an aura of sainthood about him.

"In his years of prosperity he wasn't happy. In poverty, he was blissfully content," others added. "Proof of it was that big smile and that something special he projected, like a soft light in his eyes staring at the sky."

Nobody knows for sure if the happiness Mr. John Johnson attained by giving away his wealth followed him until he died. But it's a well-known fact that, at the time of his death, the Hospital of Perpetual Assistance went bankrupt because the pathetic members of the administrative council and the board of directors, rotten by greed, had sifted through the funds entrusted to them by the altruistic multimillionaire for care of the city's poor. One of the board members had issued checks for non-existent persons and later cashed them himself. Another wrote checks addessed to firms that cooperated gladly in the fraud. Most of them didn't even make an effort to hide their dishonesty. The mistresses and wives of the reputed upright executives cooperated enthusiastically to their money-sucking operations, which in the shortest stretch of time devoured the most efficient health care center in the world and, of course, as usual, the victims were the poor who were deprived of the right to health.

The good intentions of the former multimillionaire — probably already welcomed in the kingdom of heaven with beatific chantings in his praise — left a host of corrupt executives in the jails of the kingdom of Earth. They were all upstarts who, when selected to climb to positions of leadership and assume responsibility for the management of millions, loudly praised the virtues of distributive justice, proclaimed their Christian beliefs, equalitarianism and a whole series of isms. But greedy for power, wealth and material possessions, they dismembered the body that protected the health of the poor, shared the slices among themselves and devoured them without sparing a single bone. Fortunately jails still exist.

"But jail sentences are always short for the rich and long and endless for the poor," lamented an old man.

All that was heard during the trial were insults to the greedy and praises to the late multimillionaire Mr. John Johnson. Only one astute economist commented.

"We live mostly concerned about our guilt toward the poor, or our pity for them, rather than about the poor themselves.

A sophisticated and skilled snoop who liked to contradict the Gospel for the heck of it, concluded.

"The biggest sin is not committed by those who pocket money that belongs to others, neither by those who despoil the poor. The biggest sin is committed by the one who, caring only about his salvation without concern for anyone else, climbs (or pretends to climb) into the kingdom of heaven.

More short stories by Rima de Vallbona in:

When New Flowers Bloomed: Short Stories by Women Writers from Costa Rica and Panama, also published by Latin American Literary Review Press.